The Many Kinds of Dirty

by Dale-Marie Bryan

amicus readers

Ideas for Parents and Teachers

Amicus Readers let children practice reading informational texts at the earliest reading levels. Familiar words and concepts with close photo-text matches support early readers.

Before Reading

- Discuss the cover photo with the child. What does it tell him?
- Ask the child to predict what she will learn in the book.

Read the Book

- "Walk" through the book and look at the photos. Let the child ask questions.
- Read the book to the child, or have the child read independently.

After Reading

- Use the picture glossary at the end of the book to review the text.
- Prompt the child to make connections. Ask: What are some other words that mean dirty?

Amicus Readers are published by Amicus
P.O. Box 1329, Mankato, MN 56002
www.amicuspublishing.us

Library of Congress
Cataloging-in-Publication Data
Bryan, Dale-Marie, 1953-
   The many kinds of dirty / Dale-Marie Bryan.
      pages cm. -- (So Many Synonyms)
   ISBN 978-1-60753-509-6 (hardcover) -- ISBN 978-1-60753-539-3 (eBook)
   1. English language--Synonyms and antonyms--Juvenile literature. I. Title.
   PE1591.B7633 2013
   428.1--dc23
                                    2013010414

Produced for Amicus by The Peterson Publishing Company and Red Line Editorial.

Editor Jenna Gleisner
Designer Becky Daum
Printed in the United States of America
Mankato, MN
12-2013
PO1186
10 9 8 7 6 5 4 3 2

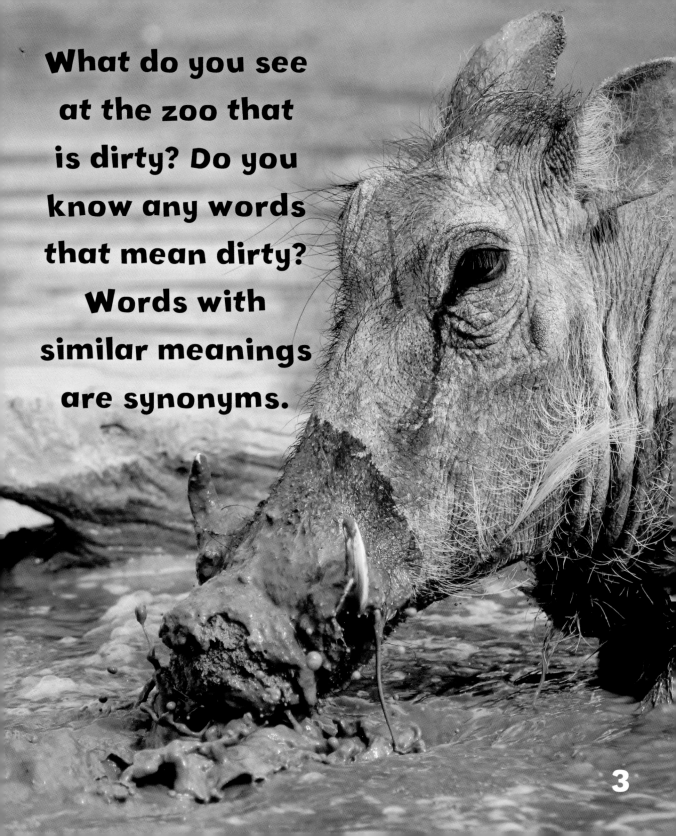

What do you see at the zoo that is dirty? Do you know any words that mean dirty? Words with similar meanings are synonyms.

4

Dusty means dirty.

Rhinos are dusty after resting in the dirt. They rest in the afternoon when it is hot.

Messy means dirty.

The zoo is messy after orangutans eat. They throw banana peels on the ground.

Sloppy means dirty.

Panda bears are sloppy when they eat. They lie on their backs and eat bamboo shoots.

Murky means dirty.

Flamingos stand on one leg in murky water. The water has lots of mud in it.

Grimy means dirty.

Elephants spray grimy water over themselves with their trunks. The grimy water keeps them cool.

13

Filthy means dirty.

Zookeepers are filthy at the end of the day. They have stains on their clothes and dirt on their boots. It is time to clean up and go home!

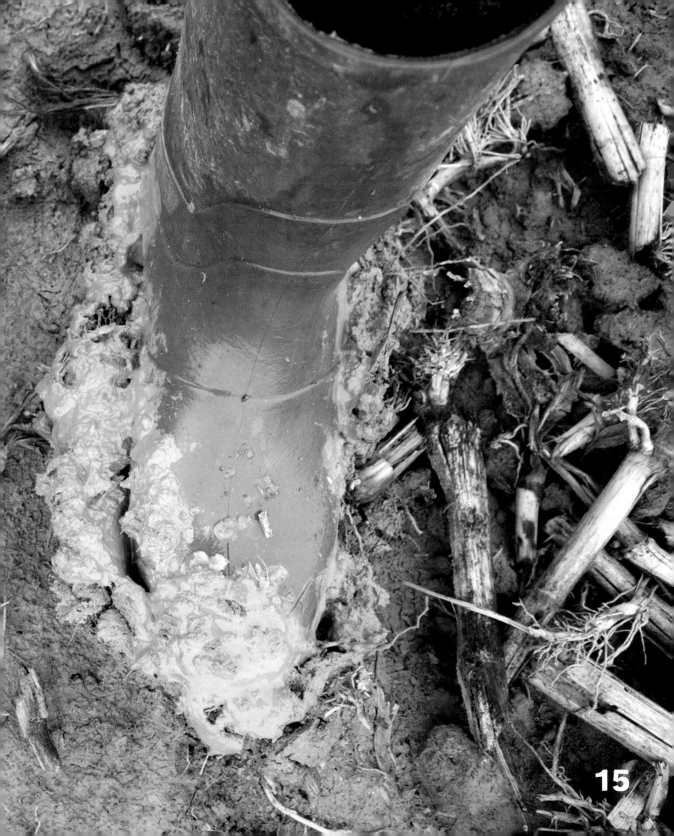

15

Synonyms for Dirty

dusty
dirty with dust

murky
cloudy

messy
out of order

grimy
sticky with dirt

sloppy
untidy

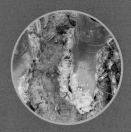

filthy
very dirty